Last Ups

Scott Morro

PublishAmerica
Baltimore

© 2005 by Scott Morro.
All rights reserved. No part of this book may be reproduced, stored in a retrieval system or transmitted in any form or by any means without the prior written permission of the publishers, except by a reviewer who may quote brief passages in a review to be printed in a newspaper, magazine or journal.

First printing

ISBN: 1-4137-7676-0
PUBLISHED BY PUBLISHAMERICA, LLLP
www.publishamerica.com
Baltimore

Printed in the United States of America

For Brion, who made growing up fun. Thanks, little bro.

For Connor and Ryan, my heroes…Daddy loves you!

For Lisa, whose support, encouragement, and suggestions throughout the process of Last Ups *were as amazing as she is. What would I do without you?*

Acknowledgments

* The Epilepsy Foundation of Landover, Maryland, for providing information on seizures and the disease when my memory from childhood failed me. Thanks!

* Doctors Richard & Stanley Stein and Dr. Martha Lusser, for their care and dedication to my brother, Brion, and their other patients who suffer from epilepsy. You make life easier.

* Meg Phillips and everyone at PublishAmerica for giving *Last Ups* and me a chance…Thank you!

~ Chapter 1~
The Longest Seven Minutes of My Life

    In exactly seven minutes, the final bell would be ringing summer vacation into existence. Gone would be the droll lessons on integers and fractions for our math and homeroom teacher, Mr. Hatcher. Gone would be conjugating verbs and writing silly poems about astronauts and spaghetti for our English teacher, Miss Reimer. I'd be rid of Becky Martin and her chubby finger, poking me constantly to ask stupid questions or to just plain annoy me. She drove me nuts! I would be free like the wind. Free to roam the neighborhood on my bike with my friends from sun-up, till the streetlights flickered and popped to life at dusk. Free to play ball till we were sore and weary, limp like a rag. Summer would be a chance to relax and be as worry-free as a child could be. Little did I know how different life would be once school let out and the stress of the "incident" would choke the life out of my happy little existence.
    "Well," Mr. Hatcher started, "I'd like to thank you all for a fun and interesting year. We worked hard together and..."
    I knew this was my cue to check out of reality for a moment and wander through the titanic list of things my friends and I would do this summer. There'd be baseball in the field near Anthony's nana's house and freeze pops across the street at Bruno's Market. We'd play bike tag and swim at the pool. And did I mention baseball? Actually, we called it tennis ball because we played with a tennis ball and a wiffle ball bat with the top cut off. We stuffed the top with bits of a Nerf football for added juice. Man, you shoulda seen the

balls fly out of Lone Star Field. It was totally cool. This was going to be the greatest summer ever!

"So, enjoy yourselves, be safe and stay out of..." *RRRRIIIINNNGGG!*

Ah, saved by the bell, I thought.

"See ya', Mr. H.," I yelled, my hand waving good-bye as I lurched for the classroom door, ready for freedom. Mr. Hatcher was a great teacher, loads of fun, but the guy had a way of making even patient people lose their patience with his constant rambling. Mr. Hatcher continued to ramble on his summer words of wisdom as we sped by him, buzzing and maneuvering our way to the exit.

In my head I was thinking, *Geez, dude, shut it off already. Schools over.* I tuned him out like the country music channel on my dad's car radio.

The typical high-fives and good-byes followed me down the annex steps and around the side door railing out the door to meet Ant, Goose, and my little brother, Brian. We had walked home everyday from school for the past five years, and this day would be no different.

As we walked, our voices melted together like ingredients in a large salad, while around us, cheers, hoots, and hollers blended with the humming of bus engines and the laughter of children.

Sounded great, right? Sounded like summer in the West End is an electrifying thing, huh? Well, usually. But not that summer. That summer was about to be a total drag, like when your Aunt Bertha, who has the big mole on her chin the size of Kentucky, tries to kiss you and pinch your cheeks till they're sore and fiery red at family reunions. That summer, I was about to get into the biggest neighborhood wedgie a kid has ever gotten into. And all of it thanks to the nightmare known as my little brother.

~ Chapter 2 ~
Spring Street's Version of Bert and Ernie

My nine-year-old brother, Brian, was an enormous pest. On the pest scale, he measured a whopping 45 out of 10. Brian was constantly repeating everything thing I said, as if he was some demented parrot with a sick sense of humor.

"Mom, he's doing it again."

"Mom, he's doing it again," the little voice would squeak with an evil grin from behind the sofa.

"Brian, that's enough. Stop annoying your brother. And Scottie, try to be more patient with him. He's younger than you are and telling him that the slimy green booger monster under his bed will eat him if he bothers you again isn't helping your situation."

A small, sinister smirk crept over my face as I turned from my mom and headed to my room to oil my baseball glove. I oiled the leather glove at least once a week, as I didn't want the valuable tool's surface to crack or become brittle from the long, hot days soaking up the sun in Lone Star Park.

I was very particular about the neatness and care of all of my things but most especially of my beloved baseball equipment. I was the Neatness Nerd, as my friends called me. My room contained the usual kid's stuff like posters and music, but my room was different than most kids in a big way. In my friends' rooms, clothes were sagging out of drawers and heaped in piles on the floor. Not mine. I had things neatly folded and placed in their proper spots. My friends called it sick. My parents called it weird. For me, it was normal. I kept things like this because of Brian.

Brian and I shared a room because our house was rather small and only contained two bedrooms, the second of which was used by our parents. As the Neatness Nerd, sharing a room was *not* cool. It was like sharing a used tissue or living inside a city dump. I hated messes, and my brother was a mess. His junk was all over the place. Clothes, toys, magazines, music. You name it; it was littering floor like confetti after the Macy's Day Parade. Brian was a slob, and I was trapped like a rat in his pigsty. I was being suffocated in my own room by the heaping mounds of clothes and the stench of dirty gym socks was making my nose weep with pain.

"Hey, stink bomb," I yelled. "You wanna tidy this up, or are dust monsters gonna grow out of that pile and engulf our room in one bite?"

"Mom!" Brian yelled. "Scott's trying to scare me again."

"The only thing scary in this room is your mess, turd boy. Clean it up!"

"Stop calling me turd boy!" Brian screamed. "You know I don't like that."

"Ok, turd boy," I sarcastically replied. "I'll stop, if you clean up. Deal?"

"Deal," Brian answered. And a momentary truce was reached. I told you sharing a room was murder.

Brian and I got along ok, but like most brothers, we had our share of fights and disagreements. Mostly, it was my fault because I was a neat freak and tormented the heck out of Brian with comments and lies about booger monsters and dust demons, and Brian was the polar opposite. He was calm and easy going, not uptight like me. Also, he was three years younger than I was, and we found it hard to connect sometimes. Not that three years was a major difference. I know we're not talking about dog years, now, but there were times when a mature 12-year-old guy like me needed to be with his friends and hang out and not play babysitter to a turd. But, that's exactly what I did every summer when my friends and I would gather across the street at Lone Star Field to play our beloved tennis ball.

"Mom, I'm going to play ball with the guys," I shouted up the stairs to my mom, who was busy making beds and tidying up. Guess where my neatness gene comes from?

"Take your brother," she called down to me, as I was trying to slink out the backdoor unnoticed.

Foiled again, I thought to myself. Just once I'd like to escape the asylum, and leave the lil' inmate with the warden. Seemed like that day wasn't going to be any different than all those days before.

As we ran towards Lone Star, the soles of our shoes burning rubber on the asphalt like an Indy car, I reminded my little bro of the rules.
"Remember, don't whine if you make an out; play hard; and most importantly, don't break anything!"

As big a slob as my brother was, that's how clumsy he could be, too.
I remember the time Brian got the Play Doh Fuzzy Pumper Barber Station for his fourth birthday. He and my Grandpa Joe had carefully taken each piece out of the box and assembled the mini-salon with Army-like precision. It shined that new-plastic shine and was in great working order once the batteries were added. It was a cool toy, and many of Brian's friends in attendance were envious of the gift. That envy soon faded, along with Grandpa Joe's patience, as Brian tripped over the box he tossed carelessly on the floor and pulverized the plastic scissors into a gazillion pieces. In the process of tripping and falling, Brian ripped the cord from the fake electric buzz clipper and smashed the mini plastic heads under his feet before he even had the chance to trim up the long, flowing turquoise blue hair. My parents were furious. My Grandpa Joe sat in disbelief. I just smiled and walked away. *One more mess from the room-sharing turd,* I thought.
I walked away, shaking my head, wondering how we could have come from the same body, the same family tree. I was beginning to think that maybe Brian's branch of the tree had snapped, and he had fallen out, landing on his head in a messy pile of leaves and twigs. That must be it. What other explanation could there be? One of us a messy slob, the other a cool but neurotic neat freak, both inhabiting the same room. One of us laid back, unfazed by clutter and disorganization; the other overwhelmed by order.

Brian and I were a sight to see in our little Spring Street house with white aluminum sides and black shutters. We were Spring Street's version of Bert and Ernie the puppets from PBS. The only thing missing from us were the sticks attached to our arms to make us move and a giant yellow bird for a neighbor.

In the weeks ahead, I would come to wish our neighbor *had* been a seven-feet tall, feathered friend and not the nightmare senior citizen who ruled our block with blue hair, a nasally voice, and a sense of humor reminiscent a Nazi prison guard. "Nosie Rosie" as we called her, was a tyrant, a 68-year-old neighborhood bully who swallowed up bats, balls, and other odd toys that landed in her yard like a giant ogre with an eating disorder. And it was getting close to her next feeding!

~ Chapter 3 ~
First Pitch, Called Strike One

As Brian and I neared the field three blocks from our home, I could sense something wasn't right, but I couldn't quite place it. It was like trying to remember an answer for a math test but drawing nothing but blanks. We passed the rows of homes, neatly planted on the edges of Spring Street, but the familiar voices and sounds that usually rung into the summer air had vanished and been replaced by a deafening silence.

"Hey, Fridge," Anthony yelled to my brother, who responded with a high-five as the three of us came face to face.

Brian was called the Fridge after the NFL player, William "The Refrigerator" Perry. William Perry was a large, mountainous man, who ate more food in one day than some small third-world countries did in a year! It wasn't unusual for Fridge Perry to eat six hamburgers, four hot dogs, and eight slices of pizza and wash all that goodness down with a Diet Pepsi in a single eating. Talk about indigestion! A case of Tums or Rolaids would help about as much as a toilet paper umbrella in a hurricane. Brian was not anywhere near as large as the "real" Fridge, but he was overweight and husky, as my Grandma Lucy liked to call him. Husky made him sound somehow older, more mature, if it's possible to be a mature, messy nine year old. Husky created a mental picture for me of a fat guy in a flannel shirt and work boots, emptying garbage cans for a living. This was certainly not my little turd brother, though being near garbage and messes certainly fit.

"Where is everyone?" I asked Anthony, who was visiting his nana as he did every day during the summer.

"Beats me," he replied in his sarcastic voice. "I didn't know it was my turn to babysit the neighborhood."

"This place is like a cemetery," I shot back at Ant.

The field was deserted. It looked like the abandoned sewing factory up the block on Wood Street. Though Lone Star Field was empty, it hardly resembled the lifeless factory a few streets away.

The Atlantic Sewing Company building had closed shop in the late 1970s, and the red brick building had remained empty ever since. Its windows were shattered and busted, like the teeth in an over rotted Halloween pumpkin. The ones that weren't broken were boarded up, like the doors, so that no one would trespass.

"Those weenies know we play at 9:30 everyday. What's up with them?" Anthony wondered aloud.

We stood a few minutes longer, staring at nothing, waiting for the others to show up. We chatted about the Reds' game the night before and the two long home runs hit by Chris Sabo, their goggle-wearing third baseman. Finally, our patience worn thin and the eagerness to play vaporized into the thin, muggy June air, we decided to head home and try and scrounge up a game after supper.

Strike one in the at-bat known as summer vacation, I whispered silently to myself, hoping strikes two and three would never materialize.

~ Chapter 4 ~
Strike Two

    Strolling home, Brian suggested that we play ball in our back yard. It would be a good warm up for the game that was sure to happen later on; plus, there was nothing to do except watch Mom do laundry and iron jeans and t-shirts. Thrillsville, right?
    For some reason, our mom was always ironing clothes, especially ones that weren't supposed to be ironed. She was like some robotic misfit creation from outer space with that steaming iron always pressed into her hand, her fingers gripping the black rubbery handle for dear life. T-shirts, jeans, panty hose, the woman would iron our underwear if we turned our backs for a second. Trying to put on a pair of Fruit of the Looms with a mammoth crease in the middle is embarrassing. Taking my clothes off and climbing into my shorts for gym class, I looked like a giant paper airplane in my tidy whiteys.

    Brian and I dropped off our junk in the living room, grabbed our wiffle ball and bat from the hall closet, and climbed the creaky wooden stairs from our kitchen door down onto the sidewalk that leaned into our one-car garage.
    Crammed within the sidewalk's borders was our yard, which measured about the size of a large postage stamp. Our yard was our *field of dreams* when the others couldn't play at Lone Star. It took our dad approximately seven minutes to weed whack and mow the grass and that was when it was actually high enough to cut.
    The neighbors laughed and joked with my father when he bought the gas-powered Toro mower at the hardware store, saying that renting a llama or goat from Donohoe Farms would be cheaper.

Janet from the next door would shout, "Hey, neighbor, don't get hurt," each time my dad would pull the motor cord and spark the engine to life.

"That's harder than the pushing," my dad would always reply with a smile.

It was a corny joke between them, and it happened without fail each time that my father cut our grass. We'd just rolls our eyes and mouth the words mockingly, shifting our heads from side to side, as we knew the stupid banter by heart.

The little turd and I strolled into the yard and got ready to play. "The beating is about to begin, turd boy," I quipped as we figured out who would hit first.

"Mom!" Brian began to scream but stopped when I flashed him a fake, but dramatically convincing "I'm sorry" smile.

We flipped a coin, and as always, I chose tails. "Tails never fails," Anthony would always say as we chose ups in the field.

It was a huge deal to choose ups. Getting last at-bats was like winning the lottery in our neighborhood. It was better than free pizza delivered to your house each week for a year. It was almost better than no homework for a month, but no teacher was that crazy to allow that to happen. Hitting last in a game meant you had the chance to shut down your opponent in their first at-bat, while giving your team the chance to come back if you were losing going into the last inning.

"Tails never fails," I repeated to the little turd as the quarter spun and flipped like an Olympic gymnast through the air, plummeting downward to the grassy landing below. When it hit the grass, the quarter did some type of twisting pretzel trick and rolled on its side for a few seconds before stopping dead and landing on heads. *Lucky me,* I thought to myself. *Do I have a sign around my neck that says, "I'm a weenie, pick on me?"*

"I want last ups," chirped the little booger to my left as he grabbed the ball from my hand and started for the back porch, which was the pitcher's mound.

"You can have last ups, turd boy. You're gonna need it," I said, stomping to home plate situated on a concrete slab that once provided a supportive base for an out house that stood on the spot before indoor plumbing was used in my home.

I was in a blind rage, steam pouring from my ears like an erupting volcano, at the way my day was turning out.

Summer vacation was supposed to be fun and exciting; yet, even though we were only one day into it, it appeared that someone forgot to share that little tidbit of information with fate on my behalf. I was drowning in Dorkville and the only life raft to safety, baseball, was frayed and slipping away from me because most of my friends had failed to show at the Lone Star season opener.

I curled the long, yellow wiffle ball bat in my hands as I stared out towards my brother, who was winding up, hurling the first pitch in my direction.

As big a pain as Brian was, the little turd could pitch. As we were growing up, my father, who was a pretty good athlete, had not only shown us both the fundamentals of baseball but the art of pitching.

In between pounding fielding and hitting skills into our heads like a drill sergeant in Spring Street Boot Camp, he took the time to show us proper grip and finger positioning on various pitches. Dad would say that too many kids get sore arms because their arms aren't fully developed and don't know the right way to throw curve balls, sliders, or change ups.

Dad was a great teacher as evidenced by the slow, arching curve ball descending from Brian's right hand and into the strike zone of our back yard.

I let this offering go more out of surprise than honest, good-eye pitch selection. The curve my brother threw caught me off-guard and buckled me at the knees. "Nice bender, bro. Hang that weak junk again, and I'm gonna deposit it in the front yard."

The matchbox-sized field we played in stretched to only 15 feet wide, while it was a mere 18 feet long, with our back porch roof standing just 12 feet off the ground. Hitting a ball on the roof or over the roof into our front yard for a homer was about as difficult as smashing an egg with a sledgehammer.

Brian smiled, though I doubt it was at my comment. He nodded in mock agreement and wound up, hurling the white plastic orb straight at the heart of home plate. The ball sped to me with missile-like velocity, again, crossing up my timing, as I was expecting another breaking pitch.

I reacted to the fastball with an equally rapid swing, sending the ball screaming out of the yard. Only, the ball wasn't headed onto the roof or over the house for a homer. It was headed straight for the multi-colored stained glass kitchen window of Nosie Rosie's house.

Like a bullet locked in on its target, our ball sped for the window like a flash of lightening, barreling on a course of destruction and doom.

At that moment, everything around us slowed to a snails pace. What took a matter of nanoseconds in reality had lasted longer than a shuffleboard tournament at an old age home. Time stood still as the little plastic ball shattered the window with a deafening scream and crashed my hopes of any fun at all for the remainder of the summer. *Strike two!*

~ Chapter 5 ~
God Bless Atlantic City Bus Trips

"What was that?" Mom yelled out the kitchen window, which was open to let fresh air in and evil dust out. Brian and I stood frozen in time, as if in a coma, petrified with fear and shock. "What *was* that?" Mom shouted again, this time, her voice breaking the ice off of our senses, loudly shaking us back to reality.

Before either the turd or I had a moment to utter a sound or offer an explanation, Mom was down the back stairs like a starved cheetah on a gazelle in the African wilderness. We hadn't seen her move that fast since a basket of folded ironed t-shirts tipped over and was about to shower the floor. If not for her cat-like reflexes, the iron would've steamed overtime that day.

When Mom came out into the yard and surveyed the damage, she shook her head and just glared at us with her piercing gray eyes. "If your father and I have told you once, we've told you a thousand times about playing ball in the back yard. It's way too small for the both of you to play back here. You're too big, and we warned you this could happen. When will you listen to us?"

Her voice droned on and on, and I tuned it out the way I did Mr. Hatcher's the morning before. I was startled back to reality by my mother's silence momentarily, before I asked, "What did you say?"

"I said, you're lucky that Rose and Thom aren't home today," Mom replied in a stern voice. "They're on a bus trip to Atlantic City with their senior club friends and won't be back until tonight. So, why don't you go over there and clean up the glass that's fallen onto the patio and sweep up. Be careful not to cut yourself, and we'll talk about how to fix this when your father gets home."

What she really meant was, "Go clean up that mess, buster, and be ready for the loudest lecture of your pathetic little life when your dad finds out what you did!"

Yeah, real lucky, Ma, I thought to myself as I moped over the small chain link fence which separated our yards, and headed for disaster number two of my day and summer vacation. At this rate, I was wishing school was about to start just to keep me sane.

Then, just when I thought it couldn't get any worse, I was dealt yet another crushing blow. My mom motioned for the turd as she was heading back into the house to vacuum for the eighth time that morning. "Where's he going?" I wondered aloud.

"Inside for snack and to play until lunch time," Mom replied confusingly as if I had 12 heads or just begged for a million dollars.

"That's not fair!" I screamed from Rose and Thom's yard. "He was playing with me; in fact, it was his stupid fault in the first place. If he hadn't thrown the ball, I wouldn't have hit it, and *we* wouldn't have broken the window!"

But my argument fell on deaf ears as Mom and turd boy disappeared behind the railing and up the back steps into the kitchen. *Nothing like kicking a dog while he's down,* I thought as I grabbed a broom and dust pan and began cleaning up the shattered pieces of the window and my summer dreams.

The clean up effort was tiring, as pieces of the bright and shiny shards of glass showered over every inch of Rose and Thom's slate-colored patio. Slivers and chunks of the once-beautiful window were loitering about on hanging baskets, patio furniture, and the nearby lawn, as though thrown there by some careless passerby. I took my time cleaning and returning the patio to its near pristine form, all the while becoming more irate at the thought of Brian inside the house, relaxing like a king, while I was sweating my brains cleaning up a mess that both of us made.

With each passing minute, I thought of ways to pay the little turd back. *Should I crush his favorite toys into meaningless rubble and powder? Nah, not severe enough. Dare I dismantle his side of the room and scream for Mom like a banshee? Nope.*

My luck, I'd get yelled at and be forced to clean it up. Plus, the mess would just drive me more insane, and at this point, I needed that like I needed a flaming case of diaper rash.

I devised evil, sinister plans of revenge that I would enact on that little monster while he was sleeping, but I hopelessly realized that his ear-piercing screams would wake me, and I'd find myself only plunging further into the depths of my parent's unfair discipline practices. I conjured up ways to break his toys or even better, get him into as big a mess as he'd gotten me into.

But how? Where? With what? I would have to be as sly as a hungry fox. I'd have to plan with military precision. This would have to be more colossal than the dilemma I was currently in. One false move, one carelessly forgotten aspect, and my goose would be cooked, forever banished to the Alcatraz that would become my existence. If this were going to happen, I'd have to move with the stealth of a cat burglar and the cunning of Sherlock Holmes.

I continued to work meticulously on Rose and Thom's porch, cleaning up the remaining bits of window when I heard our back door squeak open and footsteps tread lightly down the wooden planks.

My mom crossed our yard and neared the fence telling me it was time for lunch. I could tell she wasn't mad anymore, as the fire that was stoked before had died down and was replaced with a sort of understanding compassion. Though she didn't actually come out and say it, I knew from her body language and demeanor that she felt bad for me. Not bad enough to bail me out with the neighbors or send my little brother out to help, but she was sympathetic.

The clean up effort I was imprisoned with actually brought me some solace and gave me time to clear my head.

Though I alone was saddled with the massive janitorial task, I was thankful for the quiet time, because when Rosie the Hun, Thom the Terrible, and my short-fused father found out about the broken window, hordes of people would cower and melt into the fetal position throughout Spring Street and probably Northampton County at the riot-like bellowing of these three unhappy individuals. Fortunately for me, it was only 12:30 in the afternoon, and I'd have plenty of time to formulate some type of verbal explanation in my defense. Dad wasn't due in from the post office until 5:30 and the Nazis next door, even later.

Thank God for Atlantic City bus trips.

~ Chapter 6 ~
A Man with a Plan?

It wasn't too long after lunch that I'd begun formulating brilliant plan after brilliant plan to snag the *chosen one* into a heaping mousetrap of trouble.

Most ideas were risky and malicious, beyond anything that had ever entered my brain before. I knew that whatever I chose would come to destroy my image and credibility in the eyes of others, especially my parents, who trusted and relied on me with their undying confidence. But I was desperate and too blinded by self-pity and rage to notice it then.

I'd always been the responsible one, the first-born, the role model. But I resolved myself to some action whatever that would be and set about plotting the revenge of the Neatness Nerd.

As Brian sat finishing his ham and cheese, I thanked him for his generous offering to help me clean up the broken pieces of Rose and Thom's window. Brian smirked and flashed a wicked little grin. He may have had Mom and Dad wrapped around his fingers like a dog taking its owners for a walk, but he wasn't fooling me.

"Just wait, turd boy," I said to him as I got off the couch and headed to my room. "You're gonna get yours."

He nodded as he did in the backyard before delivering the fateful pitch that destroyed the window, having not a care in the world. And why should he? He had Mom and Dad on his side and was untouchable by the neighbors, as I, technically, was the one who hit the ball. And I, technically, was the brother who was supposed to know better. And, I technically could give a rat's butt about it all. Brian was about to find out what life was like as a scapegoat. And it wasn't going to be pretty.

My mind raced as hundreds of devious and over-the-edge ideas filled my brain. Cutting the brake line on his bike was a start, but I realized hurting him physically was not what I wanted or needed.

The pay back needed to be something subtle, something that could look accidental, something that would not point a guilty finger at me. And sliced brakes would aim a flashing neon arrow in my direction and practically drop the proverbial smoking gun into the palm of my hand. Bad idea.

Setting Brian up to break some of Mom's expensive Waterford crystal glasses that she'd gotten as a wedding present was my next bright idea, but I later decided against that, too. Mom would be the one who'd suffer and agonize most over the delicate glassware's demise, not Brian. And the last thing I wanted was to hurt Mom. Though she did play an integral part in Brian's escaping justice, I wanted no part of anything further aggravating my parents.

No matter what plan I formulated, I dismissed it almost immediately for one reason or another. Nothing I could think of would produce the end result I was so desperately searching for: Brian in trouble, and me soaking up the rays of innocence. Each moment that passed brought me dangerously closer to the brink of obsession. I was making myself mental, and I knew that if I didn't snap myself out of this dismal funk soon, I'd make another monumental error in judgment and make matters worse for myself, though I seriously doubted that was possible.

Whatever I was planning would have to come subconsciously, on the spur of the moment.

I calmed myself considerably by taking deep breaths and turning on my stereo. The music helped drown out my thoughts, and I closed my eyes, hoping to settle the last bit of nerves that were spiraling out of control.

As the last bit of frustration drifted my body on the sounds exiting the stereo speakers, I was certain that whatever was going to happen would sneak up on me and announce its presence when I least expected it.

~ Chapter 7 ~
Uh Oh, Daddy's Home

Some sounds are clearly identifiable to young, teenage ears. The annoying yippy bark of Baby, Thom and Rose's poodle, was unmistakable when it woke you from a deep, sound slumber at 5:00 a.m. on weekend mornings. The frustrating nasally whine of a younger sibling as it repeatedly harasses you and makes you wish you were deaf is distinctive, in its own nerve-wracking way.

However, eerily recognizable those things may have been, none terrified my heart with more fear than the sputtering gasp of my father's evergreen colored Toyota as it labored up the road on its two-mile journey home from the post office.

The Green Machine, as we called it, rattled and shivered as if afflicted by hypothermia when it turned corners or reached speeds over 35 miles per hour. The vehicle was a compact mass of Japanese metal, and it was creeping up Spring Street, easing itself aside the curb in front of our home.

I spread the heavy amber-tinted curtains wrapping our front window and peeked out from behind the slit. As I saw my dad's door creak open, I flew up the stairs to my bedroom and began rummaging through my things.

Whenever I'm nervous or unsettled, I calm myself by being busy, usually flipping through my baseball card collection or listening to music. Somehow, the distractions calm my nerves and allow me to relax so I can face the anxiety head on.

My bedroom door was cracked just enough for me to hear my father come through the front door and pet our black lab, Mischa, on his way into the kitchen. There, he continued his nightly ritual of greeting Mom with a kiss to her head while she made dinner.

I could hear sounds in the kitchen below, but their hushed murmurs made it difficult to decipher. I was certain that as soon as my short-fused father learned of the morning's events, he'd erupt like Mount St. Helens and leap our staircase in a single bound, thrashing and gyrating with the propulsion of a hurricane.

What my father lacked in physical stature, he made up for with his anger and voice. "Dynamite comes in small packages, too," Anthony would always say when asked how the smallest kid on our block, the smallest kid on the field, could run so fast and hit so hard. The same theory applied to my dad, I guess. Though he only stood five feet four inches tall, my father possessed the temper of an infuriated hornet.

Here comes strike three, I thought to myself as the rest of the summer reeled before my eyes, a horror movie of my life.

I sat and gazed out the window, lost in thought as all I had hoped and prayed for all school year long was lost because of one single incident. I knew once dad heard the news, I'd be grounded until September. My bike, my baseball cards, and my freedom would be wiped out, erased with whatever fun the summer had in store for my friends and me.

I knew that Mom would try and soften the blow for me with my father because despite her neurotic cleaning and straightening up, she loved and cared for Brian and me and would do anything for us.

I was startled back to reality by tapping on my bedroom door and a somber voice that asked, "Can I come in?"

The dark cloud that hung over me this morning was bursting with inevitable trouble soon to rain down over me.

~ Chapter 8 ~
Curve Ball

When my bedroom door opened, my father walked in with his head slightly bowed down and his warm green eyes peering up at me through sympathetic brows. A small, understanding grin spread on his lips.

The forecast of gale force winds and destructive rain sputtered and stalled. Hurricane John brought no more damage that a warm breeze on a summer's day.

"Can I just crawl under my bed to hide and wait for the screaming to end?" I mumbled sarcastically.

I don't know why at such a tense moment I found the need to be a smart-alec, but adding fuel to the fire is what teenagers do best sometimes. I figured I've got nothing to lose, so why not swing for the fences with dear old Dad?

But instead of unleashing the verbal tirade I was sure was brewing inside him, my dad threw me a curve and sat down harmlessly on the edge of my bed.

With his weathered and worked hands, my dad patted the spot on the comforter next to him and nodded for me to sit.

My father slipped his arm around my shoulder, and we sat there for what seemed like hours, just nestled close to each other.

Though neither of us had said a word, I could sense my father felt as bad about the broken window as I did and was doing his part to console me.

Underneath the gruff exterior, beneath the layer of blaring voice and fiery temper, my dad was a sensitive, caring man, who loved my brother and me but had a difficult time expressing it.

I lifted my head off my father's shoulder, which had fallen there a few minutes into our embrace and sobbed uncontrollably. "It was an accident, Dad. We were supposed to play ball in the field, and none of the guys showed up, and I know we're not supposed to play ball in the yard 'cuz we're too big, and we could break something, but...and Brian was playing, too, but Mom..."

My squeaky, adolescent voice trailed off to an inaudible whimper as I buried my face deeper into the gray-blue striped postal shirt hugging my father's body. He patted my back till the tears stopped flowing, and I raised my head to speak again, but my father stopped me before I could say a word. He looked me in the eyes and spoke in an unfamiliar, calm manner.

"Your mother told me what happened here today. She told me about the mix up at the field and the ball through Rose and Thom's window. I'm not angry, but I am disappointed. You know better, and your mom and I have warned you a thousand times about something like this happening."

My father spoke, and for once, I listened. I didn't tune him out or wrestle my emotions to keep from crying. I kept eye contact and let his words soak into my brain.

When he finished, he patted my back and motioned to me. "Let's go eat. Your mother's got dinner on the table," he said. "Plus, you *and* your brother have some explaining to do to Rose and Thom."

With that, we got up and headed down the stairs. No fire works, no fanfare, no titanic shouting match. My father had treated me like a man. Like one of his peers. Like an adult. It seemed like whenever you're looking for one pitch, life up and fools you with a curve to keep you honest and on your toes.

~ Chapter 9 ~
Ding! A Round with Rosie

Forks and knives clanked against plates like ringing bells, while glasses bumped nervously into the wooden kitchen table as we ate and drank. Our conversations purposely avoided the morning's incident and the show down soon to take place when the bus from Atlantic City arrived back in town.

The chewing and slurping of food and drink melted into a tone-deaf symphony of pre-digestive noise. When someone tried to speak, his or her words were lost in the suppertime sonata.

It was Brian who spoke first, bringing a much-needed intermission to the table.

As he walked to the sink with his plate and silverware, he said confidently, "I'm going to ride my bike in the alley behind Gram and Pop's. See ya' later."

"Not so fast," Mom interrupted. "You need to go with your brother over to Rose and Thom's to apologize for their broken window."

Frozen, like a deer caught in headlights, Brian whirled on his heels and stuttered, "Wh...What? Why do I hafta go, too? He's the one who hit the ball and broke the window." His plans shattered like the window next door, Brian stood defiantly in the middle of the kitchen with his hands curled up into the "Why me?" pose.

Mom and Dad shook their heads side to side in perfect unison, bringing on an uncharacteristic outburst from my brother.

"That's not fair!" he screamed, his face red and a long vein throbbing rapidly on the side of his neck. Brian slumped angrily into his kitchen chair, defeated, fully aware he was not going to slither out of harm's way this time.

I gave him a chipper wink of my right eye as I headed to the counter to drop off my dish and fork.

Brian shot me a dreadful glance and snorted, obviously disgusted by the ironic turn of events.

It was a few minutes past seven o'clock when my parents finished the dishes, and Dad climbed the stairs for a shower.

Rose and Thom would be home any second, and Brian and I would have to weather a blue-haired wrath that rivaled our father in rage and intensity.

If my mother and father had warned us a thousand times about playing ball in the back yard, then Nosie Rosie had said it a hundred million times more. Her yard was smaller than ours, a square the size of two-ply toilet paper, centered between her white clapboard house with gray shutters and the cinder block garage.

Rose Deitrich was a typical senior citizen. She enjoyed bingo, gambling on the slots at A.C., and gardening. There was one little extra bonus that made this old lady tick: she took pleasure in making the neighborhood kids miserable!

Her thinning blue hair and wrinkled skin hung on her 68-year-old frame like a scarecrow dangling in a field of wheat. Though small and frail, she was as frighteningly imposing a figure as my father, and he was 35 years younger.

Rose treated her yard as if it were a sanctuary for endangered animals. The grass was neatly trimmed every other day with an old-fashioned push mower, complete with rotary blades that manicured the lawn with beauty shop accuracy.

The grass sprouting from the Deitrich lawn was a faint green hue, mixed with a heavy brown color. Excessive mowing caused root damage in the summer months, as the delicate blades received no shelter from the sun's lethal rays.

Balls that landed in other neighboring yards were returned with a smile and without interference. Balls landing in Rosie's yard met certain doom and were ultimately never returned. Her yard was a cemetery for sports equipment, and God only knew how many unsuspecting rubber, plastic, or leather-covered orbs Brian and I sent to their graves.

When a brand-new wiffle ball landed in Rosie's graveyard a month ago, I bravely hopped the fence and attempted to retrieve it. Before I could snatch it from her dentured jaws, she came down her back stairs and into the yard after the ball as if she'd yelled "Bingo" and was headed up the aisle of the Senior Center to collect her prize.

Arthritic hip and all, the old lady beat me to the ball and jammed it in her pocket like an infant hiding a toy. I flashed a sarcastic grin and held out my hand, waiting for Rosie to deposit it in my palm. But instead of returning the ball, she turned and hobbled back towards her door, shaking her head from side to side, mumbling, "Oy, oy, oy...these kids."

Whenever she got angry or disgusted at something, Rosie would utter the subtle "Oy, oy, oy" phrase.

Brian and I used to think it was cool and would repeat the inane expression when we were younger. Whenever anything bad happened or a grown up did something we thought was wrong, "Oy, oy, oy" came out of our mouths while our fingers wagged back and forth, expressing disapproval.

At first, our parents and Rosie thought it was cute, but soon, it began to grow on Mom and Dad's nerves like a flesh-eating fungus, and they put a stop to that faster than the turd and I could say "Oy!"

I never did get that ball back or any other, for that matter. They just disappeared inside Nosie Rosie's house and vanished forever.

What she did with them all, I'll never know. Maybe she gave them to the homeless shelter for underprivileged kids. Maybe she traded them for extra Bingo cards on Thursday nights. Or maybe, just maybe, she and Thom played a geriatric World Series in their basement when us kids went in for the night. Each of them taking turns batting our wiffle balls with a cane, speeding to old couch pillow bases in wheelchairs, while Baby the pooch cheered them on.

Whatever their fate, I wish my little plastic friends well.

Dad came down the stairs, fresh from his shower, and motioned with a calling wave for Brian and I to follow him.

Like little lambs to the slaughter, we followed, keenly aware our execution waited just beyond the fence in our back yard.

We walked in single file, I behind my father and Brian behind me. The turd and I were hanging our heads, ashamed, embarrassed, and looking for the slightest bit of mercy.

The Deitrich kitchen door was slightly ajar, and I could hear faint sobs mixed with the sweeping noise of a dustpan and brush.

My father gently rapped on the door, and Thom appeared, his somber face pressing against the screen.

"John," Tom said, nodding his head soberly as he lifted the latch, opening the door.

"My boys have something they need to say to you and Rose," replied my father, ushering us into the tiny kitchen, drunk with the odor of sadness.

Brian and I stood, anxiously huddled next to each other, practically climbing into the back pocket of our father's faded Levis. Rosie looked up from her spot on the floor, sweeping up the last of the debris that had fallen inside.

Her eyes, big and round, like that of a hoot owl, were clamped on us like the jaws of a steel trap. As she began to speak, a tiny tear floated down from her eye and landed upon her rouge-colored cheek. "I'm disappointed in you boys," she spoke shakily. "Who's going to pay for my window?"

Brian and I stood dumbfounded, mute. Unable or unwilling to speak, we just stood there lost in childhood awkwardness, soaking up the barrage of rhetorical questions and lecturing being fired at us.

Afraid to look up or speak for fear the wooden handled brush might crash into our legs or the sides of our rear ends, we stood speechless.

Though Rosie would never have laid a hand or wooden sweeping instrument on either of us, at a tense moment like this, no one could ever be sure what the hysterical reaction of a senior citizen might be.

Rosie had stopped the verbal attack long enough for my father to offer his own apology and assurance that the window would be repaired and at no cost to my elderly neighbors.

My father then turned to Brian and I as a signal it was our turn to apologize and offer an explanation of what had happened earlier that day.

As the oldest, I figured I should ante up and speak first. Like both my parents had said, I was the big brother, and I should've known better. I had let the disappointment of the Lone Star mix up obscure my judgment. But as I opened my mouth to speak, I was interrupted by the dull thudding noise of my brother falling to the floor.

Lying still, as if he had fainted, Brian's skin was cool and clammy. His eyes were rolling rapidly back into their sockets while his body began to shake in tiny jolts on Rose and Thom's kitchen floor.

Broken windows and baseball games no longer mattered as Brian continued his spastic movements on the rug. Suddenly, offering apologies and deciding who and how the broken window was being paid for or repaired wasn't as important as my brother's condition. Everything else took a back seat.

Still reeling from Rosie's lecture and the frightening scene that played out before me with Brian, I was sluggish in responding to my father as he urged me to speed next door for my mom and help.

We arrived back across the fence in a blur of arms and legs, practically wrestling each other to get in Rose and Thom's kitchen door first. Mom managed to squeeze past my thigh and inch her way to my brother, still helpless on the floor.

She turned Brian on his side and moved his head carefully, raising his chin and opening his mouth, moving his tongue so he wouldn't choke on it during the seizure.

Instead of worrying about how much trouble we were in or how we were going to pay for the damages, I suddenly began to worry whether or not my brother would be around to see any of it at all.

And the most ironic thing of all was I thought *I'd* be the one down for the count when this whole ordeal started, *not* Brian. Guess I was wrong again.

~ Chapter 10 ~
Sirens and Nightmares and Scares, Oh My...

In the blink of an eye, EMT services were racing down Spring Street with sirens whining and red lights flashing their cautious warnings to cars and pedestrians alike.

Neighbors on both sides of the street, including my grandparents who lived three doors away, were out on the sidewalks gawking and whispering with curiosity.

Inside Rose and Thom's kitchen, Brian was groggy, awakening from the spasms that rendered the room silent. Not clear about what had happened or why he was flat on his back in the middle of Nosie Rosie's kitchen, Brian sat up with the help of two EMTs.

Sitting upright with his back leaning against a set of wooden cabinets, Brian's forehead was dabbed with a cool rag by my mother while one EMT checked his vital signs. He shone a mini penlight in Brian's eyes and checked his pupils. He asked my brother a series of easy questions about the alphabet, the day of the week, his name, and other questions that seemed rather unimportant to me.

Little did I know then, that the EMT was checking my brother's memory recall and brain function.

Satisfied with Brian's answers, the tech smiled and patted my brother on the shoulder, offering a reassuring touch.

The second technician interviewed my parents about the episode and made notes in a little spiral-bound notebook, while Rose and Thom stood nervously off to the side.

Rose had begun crying again, this time out of fear and worry. Thom cradled a consoling arm across her shoulder while reaching for a box of tissues with his other arm. Rose wiped the tears from her eyes and tried to listen in on the conversation between my parents and the EMT.

"We were standing here, discussing the window the boys broke earlier, when all of a sudden he flopped to the floor and began convulsing," my father offered, trying his best to act composed.

The EMT with the notebook nodded and scribbled illegibly on the tiny sheets of blue-lined paper.

After asking a few more questions of my mother and father concerning Brian's medical history and his activities for that day, the two technicians stepped out of Rose and Thom's kitchen, away from my family and two neighbors, and out to the side door of the ambulance.

They spoke in muted tones from what I could spy through the bottom part of the screen door and made several notations on a clipboard before returning into the house.

Speaking with both my parents this time, the EMTs told my mother and father that Brian had suffered what they believed to be a Grand Mal seizure, and they would need to contact our pediatrician, Dr. Stein, first thing in the morning.

My mother and father, already shaken by what transpired, seemed to tumble further into the scary unknown of helplessness.

Seeing the desperate cry for help in my parents' eyes, the EMTs carefully and with reassuring comfort explained that a Grand Mal seizure was serious and would require further consultation from a physician. They told my parents what tell-tale signs to look for should Brian have another seizure and what steps they should take during and after the episode.

Keeping my brother from falling and injuring himself was the first priority. After gently lowering him to the floor, Mom and Dad would need to gently support his head and move any furniture or sharp objects to prevent further injury.

Next, my parents were to loosen any tight clothing on Brian's body and be sure to keep Brian rolled on his side to prevent him from choking on his own vomit.

That's gross, I thought to myself, but Mom and Dad stored these important facts in their memories as a matter of life and death. Which, they were.

A bit more informed, my parents seemed to relax, and I could see the muscle-clenching tension subside in their shoulders as they exhaled a relieving breath.

Before leaving, the two technicians again checked Brian's eyes, pulse, and repeated the series of questions they had asked before. Again, my brother answered them successfully, as if nothing had ever happened and looked absurdly at the EMTs as they nodded in agreement.

As the ambulance drove away and the neighbors disappeared in the shadows of the onsetting dusk, my grandparents joined us at the back stairs of the Deitrich home, looking for answers to their heart-stopping questions.

My mother and father filled them in, along with Rose and Thom, who had now stepped back into their kitchen.

My grandmother let out a soft whimpering cry when she heard the word "seizure" but forced a smile onto her lips when she saw Brian peeking at her from the table a few feet away.

Reassuring my grandparents and neighbors that Brian was fine, my parents motioned for us and we headed towards the door and home. Mom and Dad held hands, a sight I was certain I'd never witnessed before, while I hung back walking by Brian's side.

Turning to me as we rounded the corner of the sidewalk, Brian said, "What happened to me back there?"

Unable to resist, I said a little too loudly, "Rose smacked you upside the head with the broom, and you dropped like a sack of cereal."

With that, my parents spun around and trekked towards us with heavy, determined steps.

"That's enough, Scott," scolded my father, whose non-amused eyes were boring holes into me with each passing second.

"What a horrible thing to say," my mother added with a heavy dose of displeasure saturating her voice.

"I…was…just…trying…to…" I stammered, but was cut off in mid-sentence by my father who spoke seriously again.

"This is no laughing matter, Scott! Your brother's condition is serious, and Rosie is upset enough about the window and your brother and doesn't need your sarcasm piled on top of everything else."

"I just wanted to cheer the turd up," I quipped rather bravely, considering neither of my parents were in the mood for jokes. "And Rosie couldn't hear me anyway," I continued on my strip of thin ice. "She hears as well as a pile of bricks."

Forgetting to quit while I was behind, way behind, my mother ordered me to my room with an anger in her eyes I'd not soon forget.

As I slinked up the stairs in obvious embarrassment, I flashed a quick smile to my brother, who was plopping himself into a living room chair, exhausted from the nightmare he'd encountered a few minutes earlier.

Brian smiled back, more out of pity than anything else. Then turned and focused his attention to the commercial blaring from the TV set anchored in the corner of the living room.

Closing my bedroom door I shook my head and thought to myself rather insensitively, *That boy will do anything to escape trouble.*

~ Chapter 11 ~
Guinea Pig and Scapegoat

I was awakened the following morning by the low droning hum of the vacuum gliding over our living room carpets below.

Some parents use an alarm clock or a gentle shake of the shoulder to rouse their children. My mother employed the Hoover method. *Killing two birds with one stone,* she would always reply when Brian and I asked her why she did it. It got us out of bed and allowed her the pleasure of grooming the carpets with intricate fiber patterns while ridding our house of the sinister dirt that dwelled between its fibers.

By 9:00 a.m. sharp, mom's fingers had programmed Dr. Stein's number into the phone, and she was relaying the facts of last night's events in graphic detail. She'd pause momentarily to catch her breath or answer one of Dr. Stein's questions before plunging back into the story.

Near the end of their conversation, mom was writing notes on a pad just as the EMT had done the night before. She thanked Dr. Stein for his time and told him she'd be in touch as soon as the pediatric neurologist, whoever that was, had examined Brian.

The next few days were an unrecognizable blur. While Mom and Dad ushered Brian off to the pediatric neurologist, a Dr. Lusser, then to Dr. Stein for another consultation and back to Dr. Lusser for a follow up appointment, I stayed home with my grandparents and busied myself with the neighborhood lawn cutting jobs that Brian and I had lined up before school let out.

Our list of clients included Janet next door, the Lillys across the street, Gram and Pop's yard three houses away, our own little plot of sod and, out of sheer pity from the night before to help pay for the window, Rose and Thom's palace of green.

We were paid $8 a job and split the money evenly, four bucks a piece.

Brian would usually spend his money immediately on candy or toys that he'd eventually break, while I stashed my money like Black Beard the Pirate burying treasure. My cash was usually spent at baseball card shows for Topps and Fleer rookies and some older Yankee cards that I thought looked much better than the cards we had.

Not only did I save my grass-cutting money, but I'd keep the lunch money my parents gave me for school each day and squirreled it away, too. I'd make peanut butter and jelly sandwiches and wash it down with a carton of milk and a bag of mini pretzels, which only cost me 40 cents total. A whole lunch was 95 cents. So, I pocketed 55 cents daily, which added up to a healthy $11 at the end of each month.

I figured I was still eating, and my parents didn't have to give me extra money for cards. I already had it. They thought I was being responsible with my cash flow, and I didn't feel the need to burst their bubble. It was a no-lose situation for everyone involved. No lose, that is, until Brian passed my lunch table in the cafeteria during the last week of school.

He'd been talking to his friend, Douglas, on the way to their table and noticed I had a brown-bagged lunch and not an orange tray filled with a hamburger, applesauce, and juice. With a puzzling smirk he said, "Who made that for you?"

"I did, turd boy, now why don't you and *Duh*glas mosey on back to the Girl Scout table where you belong and leave me alone!" I flung back.

Without missing a beat, Brian turned and grabbed my sandwich in one single motion and wolfed down a hefty bite. His pudgy, crayon-stained fingers engulfed my lunch and tiny bits of white bread glued with peanut butter flew like sparks from his mouth as he spoke. "This is better than Mom's," he said sarcastically. "I'll be sure and tell her what a gourmet chef you've become."

At that point, I knew I was sunk like the *Titanic*. One word of this whispered to my Mom, and I'd be mowing lawns and tackling other chores for free.

What could I say or do? The little monster *had* learned from the best, and he'd beat me at my own game. I was furious and embarrassed but had no choice but to meet his demand of half of the lunch money I'd saved so he could buy the new *Dukes of Hazzard* action figures he was salivating over. I had been hoarding my lunch money and choking down peanut butter sandwiches for about three months, so half of my take was close to $12. More than enough for Bo and Luke Duke immortalized in rubbery plastic by Mattel.

So, instead of waltzing into the Palmer Mall's annual Sports Card Expo in July with $85 burning a hole in my pocket, I was light $17 but armed with enough ammunition to pay the little turd back once and for all, as soon as the opportunity presented itself.

Brian still refused to handle the window situation responsibly, and I was furious. Even then, as he was afflicted with epilepsy and enough medical tests to make a lab rat cry, I was determined to throw sympathy and compassion aside and go forward with my revenge plan, whatever it was, even though I still had no plan at all.

For all the emotional torture my parents were dealing with on a daily basis, I never once considered their feelings or those of my brother, for that matter. I stayed locked inside my own emotional cocoon, starving myself of the reality of my brother's situation. While I was off pushing lawn mowers though yards, trimming and earning twenty bucks, Brian was enduring EEGs, electroencephalograms, with twenty or more pads stuck to various locations on his head that measured his brain activity.

When I was sprawled out on the couch, cooling off in the air conditioning with a glass of ice tea, my brother's head was trapped inside a mobile couch scanner, receiving a head CT, which took x-rays of his brain at various angles. And, as sticks or pine needles were pricking my skin when I raked them up with the grass clippings, Brian was being jabbed with syringes that took his blood for analysis, hoping to find a cause for his seizures.

Brian was a guinea pig for pathologists, pediatricians, and neurologists. Whatever tests they prescribed, he was a willing participant, ready and cordial, no matter how much it freaked it him out.

According to my parents, he never complained or even whimpered. He sat or laid down cooperatively, just hoping that the more agreeable he was, the sooner the invasion of his body would be over.

I was the scapegoat in the family, taking the heat for the broken window and accepting full responsibility for its destruction.

Despite the fact Brian and I were both involved, his current condition exonerated his accountability and left it squarely piled upon my teenage shoulders. At least that's how I felt. I'm not sure if it was guilt or pity that flooded my senses, but I was drowning in a sea of emotions, ranging from anger to sympathy and back to anger. I was angry about the broken window and having to use my baseball card money to pay for its repair. I was sympathetic to my little brother and the amount of poking and prodding he was enduring practically on a daily basis. And then I was angry again. Angry at myself for getting into the broken window mess in the first place. Angry at my friends for ditching us the morning before and causing the window thing to happen. Angry that I was angry and could nothing about it.

My parents would talk openly to me about the tests being performed on Brian, why they were being done, and the hopeful prognosis they could bring. They never brought up the window or repairing it, which I hadn't noticed in all my days of cutting, raking, and resting, had been fixed.

Apparently, Thom had gotten the materials and repaired the window himself, saving Brian and me money and my family further stress. For all their elderly quirks and annoying nosiness, Rose and Thom were pretty good neighbors. But once again, I was too blinded by my own self-pity to notice.

My parents never treated me differently, neglected me, or made me feel unimportant throughout all of Brian's ordeals. Instead of dividing their time or love, they multiplied it and made sure Brian or I hadn't changed as a result of his new challenge. They made it seem as if we weren't the guinea pig or scapegoat at all. On the contrary, they were the ones who changed.

Rather than dust the tables till the wood was practically sanded down or vacuum till the carpets were worn and frayed, Mom cleaned with a lessened sense of determination. Making each nook and cranny of our house dust free wasn't as important as making sure each facet of her boys' lives was in tact.

And Dad was practically a new man. Little things that would have set him off in the past seemed insignificant in the new larger scheme of things. His temper was no longer a raging blaze of emotions. It was nothing more than a cooling ember. Dad had gone from high strung to high-spirited in a matter of a few days.

The change in both my parents was miraculous. It was amazing how tragedy can transform body, mind, soul, and family.

~ Chapter 12 ~
A Bitter Pill to Swallow

    The gusting winds of panic and uncertainty seemed to die down a bit after Brian's initial testing was complete and some of the preliminary results returned. More than a week had passed, and Dr. Lusser had determined from the EEG, the brain scan, and the blood work that my brother indeed had epilepsy and would need to take medication to help control the seizures.
    Though Brian's condition was serious, the meds would help curtail the seizures and allow my brother to lead a fairly normal life. If by normal, she meant continuing to pester and annoy me to the point of dementia. And if by normal, she meant to continue narrowly escaping trouble like a slippery eel, then God help me.
    There were about half a dozen FDA approved medications for epilepsy on the market, but Dr. Lusser felt that Dilantin and Tegretol would work best for the little turd. What my parents had learned from their tour of medical facilities in the past three weeks was that the development of anti-seizure medications had been quite slow. The ones currently on the market were successful and effective but carried some hefty side effects.
    Dilantin and Tegretol would help control the seizures, but could produce swelling of the gums, facial hair growth, and brain atrophy over an extended period of use. Great! As if being an epileptic wasn't dangerous enough, pharmaceutical companies were trying to turn epileptics, including my 9-year-old brother, into the offspring of a Cabbage Patch kid and the Wolf Man. What next, pointy ears and howling and drooling at leafy vegetable fields? How much does one child have to endure for normalcy?

I could just see it. Brian swallows his morning Dilantin and Tegretol with a chin-dripping gulp of water, then runs and hides behind the couch, while he morphs into Cabbage Wolf Kid, medical super hero, faster than a Crawling Catherine doll, more powerful and shaggy than a Hair-Extension Barbie, able to gum soft foods in a single spooning. Oy, oy, oy! This was not gonna be pretty.

All of this might have played out according to my twisted sense of humor, had, in fact, my parents actually gotten Brian to take his medicine.

Though the little turd didn't transform into a hairy-faced, lettuce-loving mutation, he did run and hide every time the pill bottles echoed their ominous rattle.

At first, he'd just plop on the couch and sit rigid, immobile like a statute, his teeth clenched tightly. The muscles of his jaw taut and straining to remain closed while my parents coaxed and cajoled him with every known plea to man to take his medicine.

Aside from using pliers and forcing his chops open, begging and pleading like a death row inmate was their only course of action. Eventually, they wore him down with the promises of staying up later and extra sprinkles on his ice cream.

Very smooth; mission accomplished. Almost anyway. Seeing two grown-ups grovel and sell their souls to a nine year old was priceless. But that only worked for about a week.

When the luster wore off that gold nugget, Mom and Dad had to up the ante because Brian took to stowing away behind the sofa.

For a kid his size, you'd think it was impossible to get back there. Nuh-uh. Slipping back there was the easy part. Getting him *out* from behind the furniture was like pushing a watermelon through a keyhole. It wasn't happening!

As this circus act unfolded before my eyes on a daily basis, I just sat back and enjoyed the show. I'd giggle and howl like a pack of hyenas at Mom and Dad's egg-shell stroll around my brother and taking his medicine.

When I wasn't snickering or throwing gasoline onto the pill-taking fire, I was mowing my share of the lawns and Brian's, too.

Until his medications were regulated in his blood stream, Brian couldn't operate a mower or play ball or do anything. He was Bubble Boy, surrounded by the plastic protection of Mom and Dad. His sole existence consisted of vegging on the sofa or hiding behind it while our parents waited on him hand and foot.

Not only did he and my parents need to consider these factors, but they also had to scrutinize and attend to Brian's diet with vigilant efficiency. Avoiding foods with caffeine, such as cola and chocolate, was vitally important. Coffee, tea, and alcohol were also on the list, but Brian becoming a caffeine-addicted alcoholic were the least of my parent's worries.

When they weren't restricting his diet and fluid intake, Mom and Dad had to fret over Brian's stress level, increased temperature, and photosensitivity. Becoming upset or being involved in stressful situations like an argument could start a seizure.

Brian's defense system could shut down and generate the onset of the clamminess and shakes. So, too, could overheating or seeing flashing lights from the TV, a strobe light, or video games. Any of these could set off a string of dangerous neurological events and trigger a seizure. No chocolate bars, no colas, and no Atari. What next? No fresh air? No breathing? The hits just kept coming.

In between dodging them like a speeding train whenever they brought him his pills, Brian might sneak into the kitchen for a snack of dried fruit or pretzels or attempt to plug in the Atari for a round of *Space Invaders* until Mom or Dad found out, and they would remove the cables for the game unit and sent him off to read or draw.

The greatest standoff took place a few days later day. It was a Saturday morning, which meant Mom and Dad were both home, to hopefully tag-team the little turd and make the stressful situation a little less tense.

My parents had received a call from Dr. Lusser right before breakfast and been informed that Brian's levels were stable, and he could resume physical activity, even mowing the lawn.

"What a relief," Mom replied and relayed the info to the rest of us after hanging up.

A definite relief, I thought. *Maybe now he could start pulling his own weight with the yard jobs. And he had plenty of weight to toss around.*

Shortly after eating, Brian and I perched on the sofa to watch cartoons, while Mom and Dad finished up the dishes.

When he heard the kitchen cabinet open with a low moan, Brian's ears perked up in the radar position, and his eyes began to flit and blink with panic. He could've dove for cover behind the couch, but instead, he slid headlong under the kitchen table, pulling the old cane-bottomed seats in around him.

My parents were too involved in conversing about the execution of their newest plan to notice that Brian wasn't planted on the couch next to me, where he was a few fleeting minutes before. Not stunned or surprised, they stared at me with a "where now?" look in their eyes. I twisted my body around the arm of the sofa and pointed a finger in the direction of the kitchen.

As they turned, falling like dominoes into line next to each other, my parents spied Brian huddled under the table.

Approaching with soft steps, my father crouched down and knelt at eye level with my brother. "Hey, pal," Dad said softly. "Come on out. It's time to take your medicine."

He repeated this phrase several times more, each time his patience thinning and the politeness of the message strangling his vocal cords. Finally, feeling defeated and his anxiety level rising from Brian's non-reply, my father turned, face scorching in frustration, and let my mother have a crack at it.

Mom shot dad a "calm down" look and began sliding the chair closest to my brother out of the way. Mom's voice was soft, almost silent as she whispered into Brian's left ear. He turned and looked up at my mother with his teary hazel eyes and nodded. In a matter of seconds, both had emerged from under the table and were headed to the cabinet for a glass and then to the sink for water. My dad and I stared at each other in open-mouthed amazement, wondering what Mom had said to get Brian out of his self-imposed prison.

Brian swallowed his pills and skipped up to our room for his sneakers, so he could quickly mow Rose and Thom's yard. Brian seemed thrilled to be on his way, armed with his improved bill of health and reward for compliant services.

Shaking my head as disbelief and shock hovered over the room like strange meandering odor, I looked to Mom for answers.

Her teeth shone as she smirked and said, "I told him if he stopped this hiding and struggling each time he needed to take his medicine, your father and I would take him to the toy store, and he could pick out any prize he wanted."

I couldn't believe what I was hearing. My ears were burning with rage and irritation. *I* did his job and mine for the past three weeks. *I* manicured each yard carefully and with the utmost attention to detail. *I* grudgingly had to split the money *I* earned, and what did *I* get for being the responsible one?

LAST UPS

Nothing, nada, zilcherooni. As usual, I was left standing at the plate, strike three whizzing right on by.

Before I stormed out the kitchen door and onto Janet's house to mow her lawn, Mom called after me. "Look," she said, stopping me in my tracks at the door. "I know you think rewarding your brother with a trip the toy store for taking his medicine seems unfair, but honey, these medications are so important. They're keeping your brother from having seizures and keeping him healthy."

She started to sob with this last confession, but I could have cared less. Instead of feeling sympathy or relief, I fired back in my typical sarcastic teenage way.

"You're right, mom, I'm sorry! *I'm sorry* I've busted my butt for the last month, taking care of his chores and mine. *I'm sorry* I've had to fork over the money for his lawn jobs, even though *I* did all the work, while the Turd of the Year sat on his throne and surveyed the kingdom. *I'm sorry* that *I* didn't get sick, too. Maybe then *I'd* be the one getting toys and surprises and rewards coming out my butt, for absolutely nothing!"

"I see," Mom whispered, visibly upset at my latest tirade. "I'm sorry you feel that way, Scott. I really am."

Then, all of a sudden, as if someone had pulled a plug, she stopped.

The silence echoing off the kitchen walls was deafening, and I began to get choked up at what I had just done. Guess Brian wasn't the only one in our house who had to swallow a pill of some sort.

With more tears in her eyes than I'd ever seen, my mom wiped them away and said, "I'm going with your father down to Gram and Pop's and tell them about Dr. Lusser's call this morning. Tell your brother when he finishes Rose and Thom's grass to come down, and we'll go to the mall from there. I'm sorry to add to your growing list of responsibilities, but I want to get down there before they leave to go shopping." And with that, she was gone.

I felt a wave of emotions wash over and nearly drown me. First, there was flooding anger, followed by an ebb of self-pity, then strong under current of anger again. The more I stood in the doorway, the more I stewed over what had just taken place. I wasn't sure if I was angry with my parents, my brother, or myself. I just knew I was angry. Each second of the past month ticked by in slow motion, replaying words, actions and emotions for me to brood over.

When the reel reached the part of the broken widow, a bright light flashed as the ball shattered the glass and an eerie glow reflected the sun's light. At this moment, a light went off inside my head and the murky details of the revenge plot I'd been so desperately seeking were suddenly crystal clear.

Not wasting another second idling in the doorway, I dashed down the steps and hurled my body over the fence separating our yard from Rose and Thom's. Brian was standing, his shoulders slumping, while Rosie barked orders into his nine-year-old face. I felt bad enough for him to interrupt and come to his defense, but why ruin a good thing?

"Cut sideways across the grass," she bellowed. "Be sure and keep the blade on the first notch. I like a close clipping. Don't let the clippings shoot into the flowerbeds, or you'll be out here cleaning them out. Sweep the porch twice, once across this way and once across the side…"

She yammered on for a few more seconds before disappearing into the tiny Ford driven by Thom. They, too, were going shopping and wouldn't be back for more than an hour. As far as she knew, Brian would be cutting her grass and wouldn't be the wiser to my evil little plan.

When she was clearly out of sight, Brian turned to me, exhausted from the one-sided confrontation and asked, "What was that all about? I've cut her grass before; I know the routine."

"I don't know," I said honestly. "Maybe she's afraid the seizures zapped your memory, and you needed a refresher on how to mow her Nazi yard."

Brian gave a faint, uncomfortable chuckle and stared at the mower. Knowing stressful situations could trigger an episode, I broke into the next phase of my revenge plan.

"Ya' know," I said, sounding helpful and sympathetic, "Why don't you just head inside to grab your money, and I'll do the job for you. You don't need any added pressure from that old bat, and I can get this when I'm finished over at Janet's. Plus, I'll even give you all eight bucks. No need to get stressed over this little yard. You've got the mall toy store calling your name. Really, get outta here and enjoy the mall. You've earned it."

Hesitating for only a second, Brian said, "Well, if you don't mind, just this once. Then, I promise I'll take over my share starting next week. She just kept going on and on about how to cut this way and…"

"Look, buddy, say no more. What are big brothers for anyway?" I replied rather convincingly.

With that, he was off. Into the house he ran and up the stairs to our room to crack open his piggy bank and grab a fistful of dollars to buy another toy along with the one my parents had promised.

I waited a few seconds before firing up the mower and cutting Janet's meager lawn, satisfied that things were finally going to roll my way.

While I was raking up the tiny bit of clippings, I spied my parent's car sputtering past, and I knew I'd have ample time to set the next step of my revenge plan into motion.

When Janet's yard was finished, I wheeled the mower around the corner of the street and down the sidewalk into Rose and Thom's yard. With anxious fingers, I sparked the engine to life and began the final phase of my payback idea. Using the nimble strokes of an artist's touch, I steered and maneuvered the mower like Picasso, carving a *J* an *E* an *R* and a *K* length wise into the soft, narrow strip of sod. I manicured the remaining slivers of grass and stepped back to admire my masterpiece.

Daydreaming for what seemed like hours, I stood and soaked up the grand magnitude of what I had just done. With those four letters, I had resurrected my self-respect, along with every dreadful incident of the past month and relived each with a new-found purpose, as if thumbing through the pages of a morbid photo album. I had breathed a new life into my world by allowing all the unfairness thrown at me to be replaced by one single act of blind malice. With those four letters, I buried the anger and the injustice done to me, righted the wrongs, and hopefully brought some much needed heat down on my little turd brother.

I was proud of my accomplishment, proud of my plan and proud of the catastrophe that was soon to take place when Mom, Dad, and the neighbors came home.

Only what was about to happen wasn't what I had planned. Once again, life had thrown me a pitch I didn't expect to see. This one wasn't a knee-buckling curve ball like the past two, though, ones that shattered dreams and windows. This one was so unpredictably different, so unexpected. This one was a change up.

~ Chapter 13 ~
Last Ups

    The phone screaming from its perch on the kitchen wall rattled and panicked like my frazzled nerves. Each ring ushered dark ominous clouds over my head and all but drove the last nail into my proverbial coffin. At least, that's what I thought.
    Mom nodded feverishly and replied, "Uh, huh, I see…" with such rapid-fire action, I lost track of the count after a dozen or so.
    When she hung up the receiver, the racket of slamming plastic ricocheted throughout the downstairs of our home, bouncing off of walls and furniture like an errant rubber ball. She called to my father, who was parked on the couch reading the newspaper. Mom's obvious aggravation beckoned my father off his seat and he hurried himself to the kitchen.
    They huddled like a quarterback calling a play, but their whispering was barely audible. Straining to hear their hushed conversation from the living room, my senses were assaulted by my father's booming voice. "What?" he bellowed from the kitchen visibly upset. "Brian, get in here now!"
    My father continued his interrogation of Brian, who now stood before him, puzzled and confused about the sudden uproar. "What would possess you to mow the word 'jerk' into somebody's lawn? Rose and Thom have been nothing but understanding throughout the entire window and seizure ordeal and *this* is how you repay them!"
    At that moment, what I had done hit Brian like an exploding fastball popping the leather of a catcher's mitt. Realizing I had carved the word into Rose and Thom's yard and set him up for the fall, Brian smirked

appreciatively at my act of revenge. Shouldering the knowledge that I had gotten last ups on him in this game, Brian knew what he had to do.

In a matter of moments, Brian was whisked out of our home and marched over to Rose and Thom's house without explanation. He cowered like a guilty dog, his tail tucked between his legs, and his head bowed low in embarrassment. Brian slinked up the back stairs and knocked sheepishly on our neighbor's door.

Rose and Thom appeared, holding the door open for them to enter. Following behind with morbid curiosity, I crept in the open door behind my father, unnoticed by the others.

Once inside, the short eerie silence was broken by my mother who spoke as Rose was about to open her mouth. "I want the truth and want it now," she said, choking back tears and bubbling anger.

Feeling guilty and full of remorse for what I had done, I was about to spill my guts and expose the whole ugly truth when Brian stepped in and tossed that change up.

"I'm sorry I did it!" he exclaimed, staring at me as the words rolled off his tongue. Tears began flowing, and Brian rambled a series of unrecognizable words and phrases, trying to explain the callous deed.

Letting sympathy cloud their judgment, the adults patted and stroked Brian's hair with compassionate understanding.

No one spoke a word, letting several minutes of silence settle over the room like a cleansing blanket of snow. Brian lifted his reddened face and shattered the calmness like I had the window, offering an apology. "I really am sorry about the damage I caused. I'll use some of the money I've saved up and buy grass seed to fix the yard."

Rose and Thom nodded and smiled in agreement, easing the pained look trapped behind my brother's eyes.

He stood and inched toward the door, shaking Rose and Thom's hands with sincerity before loping down the steps.

Sensing my parents were going to stay and chat a few minutes longer, I trailed behind Brian and slipped out the door as easily as I had come in.

I caught up with my brother a few steps from the street corner and rested my right arm around his shoulder. "Why'd you do that...back there, I mean? Why did you take the heat for me? You could've told the truth and been off the hook."

He stopped, put his arm around my shoulder and said, "I know how much going the Card Expo means to you. If you had gotten into trouble, you would've been grounded and missed the show. I got what I wanted at the mall and figured, why not save you for a change? Remember last year playing football in the field? Goose's big brother, Matt, was picking me on. You made him knock it off and threatened to beat him up if he didn't leave me alone. I never said thanks for that and figured this was my chance."

"I thought you'd forgotten all about that once we got home," I said.

"Yeah, but I didn't," Brian replied. "You stick up for me all the time, whether it's with the bigger kids or with chores." He continued, "I...well, uh...appreciate it."

I smiled softly and said, "You're welcome, turd, you're welcome."

We continued up the street to our house, arms around each other, not saying another word.

I guess, in a way, we both had last ups that day. My last ups were through my payback plan and the freedom to enjoy the card show. Brian's last ups were earned for taking the heat for the yard mess and for sharing with me why he had done what he did. In a way, we both homered in that last at bat. In a way, we both won the game.

For the past four weeks, I thought I had toiled and slaved and weathered the storm of chores and unfairness hurled in my direction by my parents, neighbors, and even my brother.

In reality, Brian was the one weathering the storm. Dealing with a selfish brother, medication that could alter his moods and appearance, and a life-threatening disease was more than any nine year old should have to endure. But, rather than see Brian for what he was, a kind, selfless little man, I allowed my own insecurities and self-pity to blind the true picture.

Brian and I have not spoken about the broken window, the carved message in the yard, or the heart-to-heart we had on the way home from Rose and Thom's since that fateful day.

In a strange way, we've gone from being each other's biggest annoyances to being each other's best friends. Thanks to a shattered window, a critical illness, and a protective lie, I know what being a real big brother is all about.

It's funny how when life throws you a curve, you think it's the farthest thing from what you want. But in reality, it's exactly what you need.

Printed in the United States
42837LVS00007B/169-192